THIS CHRISTMAS

BOOK BELONGS TO

....

....

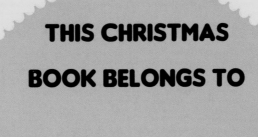

HEY DUGGEE

LADYBIRD BOOKS

UK | USA | Canada | Ireland | Australia | India | New Zealand | South Africa

Ladybird Books is part of the Penguin Random House group of companies whose addresses can be found at global.penguinrandomhouse.com.

www.penguin.co.uk   www.puffin.co.uk   www.ladybird.co.uk

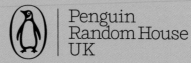 Penguin
Random House
UK

First published 2020
001

Text and illustrations copyright © Studio AKA Limited, 2020
Adapted by Jenny Landreth

Printed in Italy

A CIP catalogue record for this book is available from the British Library

ISBN: 978-1-405-94735-0

All correspondence to:
Ladybird Books
Penguin Random House Children's
One Embassy Gardens, 8 Viaduct Gardens, London SW11 7BW

TAG

DUGGEE
AND THE
CHRISTMAS
BADGE

BETTY   **ROLY**   **NORRIE**   **HAPPY**   **DUGGEE**

It's Christmas at the clubhouse!
Duggee and the Squirrels are merrily
singing a Christmassy song when the
doorbell rings . . . Who will it be?

DING-DONG!

It's Duggee's old friend Clarence.
"You haven't changed a bit!" says Clarence grumpily.
"And who are you?" he asks the Squirrels.

"We're the SQUIRRELS!" they say.
"We're getting ready for Christmas,"
say Norrie and Happy.
"It's so **EXCITING!**" shouts Roly.
Clarence doesn't sound so sure.

Duggee thinks Clarence needs a bit of
help to get in the Christmas spirit.

"Would you like a mince pie?" asks Tag.
"Not for me, thank you. They taste so same-y . . .
after the first three million," replies Clarence.

"Could we tempt you with Duggee's Festive Fruit Cup?" asks Happy.
"I suppose it might help get me through the Christmas holiday," Clarence sighs.
"But this is the best time of the year!" cries Norrie.

"I would spend *all* year getting ready.
It was hard work, but I loved it."

POOR CLARENCE.

"He's lost his Christmas cheer," says Norrie.

WE NEED TO HELP HIM FIND IT!

"By making him an extra-special Christmas!" says Betty.

BUT HOW?

First, everyone has a think. What are *their* favourite things about Christmas?

Duggee's favourite thing about Christmas is the surprises.

"I love Christmas hats!" says Happy. "Last year, I made a hat for Eric."

"I love Christmas songs!" says Tag.
"My aunty plays the piano and we all sing."

"I love Christmas food!" says Norrie. "I make a huge gingerbread house with my brothers and sisters, while Dad makes the Christmas curry."

"And at my house," says Roly, "we play
Find the Christmas Potato!"

The Squirrels get busy, hoping they can help Clarence get back his Christmas cheer.

They get out the tree decorations . . .

make hats for everyone . . .

and crackers . . .

build a gingerbread house . . .

hang up the stockings . . .

wrap presents . . .

and find a good place to hide a potato!

Meanwhile, Duggee is
very busy in the kitchen.

Clarence relaxes and chats to Enid.
"Isn't it nice, Enid," he says, "having little helpers?"

Finally, the tree is finished.
"It looks **AMAZING!**"
say the Squirrels.

AH-WOOF!

And Duggee's
flaming nut roast
is ready to eat.
It's time for . . .

. . . the clubhouse Christmas feast!

The table is crowded with delicious food and everyone is very happy, even Clarence.
"This is marvellous, Enid!" he says.

Duggee and the Squirrels have reminded Clarence that it's the little things that make Christmas special.

It's time for Clarence to go. He has lots to do!

Everyone waves goodbye.
"Why is Clarence climbing up the chimney?" asks Betty.

As Clarence flies away in his sleigh, they start to wonder . . .

Could Clarence be . . .?

Duggee, it's time to give the Squirrels a present – their **Christmas Badges!**

AH-WOOF!

Now there's just time for one more thing before the Squirrels go home . . .

"DUGGEE HUG!"

Happy Christmas, Duggee!